Blowfish live
in the sea

Paula Fox:

Blowfish live in the sea

Aladdin Books
Macmillan Publishing Company • New York

Collier Macmillan Publishers • London

Aladdin Books
Macmillan Publishing Company
866 Third Avenue, New York, NY 10022
Collier Macmillan Canada, Inc.

First Aladdin Books edition 1986
Printed in the United States of America
A hardcover edition of Blowfish Live in the Sea *is available from*
Bradbury Press, an affiliate of Macmillan, Inc.

10 9 8 7 6 5 4 3 2 1

Library of Congress Cataloging-in-Publication Data
Fox, Paula. Blowfish live in the sea.
Reprint. Originally published: Englewood Cliffs, N.J.: Bradbury Press,
1970.
Summary: Carrie's half brother Ben has long felt rejected by his father
until, on a strange visit in Boston, he is able to see that his father really
needs him.
[1. Fathers and sons—Fiction]   I. Title.
PZ7.F838B1   1986   [Fic]   86-11275
ISBN 0-689-71092-5 (pbk.)

For my brother, Bruce

Blowfish live
in the sea

One:

My brother, Ben, says that blowfish live in the sea.

He says it in many ways. I've found it written on matchbook covers, on brown paper bags from the supermarket, in dust on the windows. That makes Mama mad because you can't get window cleaners to come anymore.

He writes *Blowfish live in the sea* on the envelopes of unopened letters he finds lying on the hall table. This makes my father mad.

Ben and I have not got the same father. I live with mine. But his father is somewhere out west, the last I heard, in Santa Fe or Tucson, I forget which. I don't like to ask Ben because he says, "I don't know, Carrie," and that ends whatever conversation we're having.

Ben is six years older than I am. He'll be nineteen this summer, and I'll be thirteen in November. I don't like the sound of that—thirteen—but my friend, Abby, says it can't be worse than being twelve. Ben and I don't look at all alike except for the color of our hair and its length. Mine is down to my shoulders now, and I expect, in the next year, to have it grow to my waist.

"Quit measuring your hair, Carrie," my brother says when he catches me looking in the mirror. "It only grows when you aren't watching."

"When are you going to get your hair cut, Ben?" my mother asks him at least once a week.

Ben's answer is to shrug his shoulders. Then Mama looks at my father and she shrugs too. Then my father's face goes blank as if he were half-listening to a conversation between two people he didn't know.

When Ben came home wearing a rawhide tie around his hair for the first time, no one said anything. But my father asked me to go for a walk with him. It was after supper, and too early to take Moon for his last walk of the day. Moon was asleep by the fake fireplace in the living room; he didn't even look up when my father dangled the leash over his head.

In the elevator going down to the street floor, my father looked at Moon, who was staring at the door, waiting for it to open.

"Moon looks like a dust spider," he said.

I'd always liked Moon's fur. When Mama has one of her big cleaning days, and the apartment ends up looking like a furniture store window, in comes Moon, the walking dust spider, with four skinny brown legs to keep him going. I can't see Moon's eyes because of his fur, which covers them entirely. Once, when I was using a doll's brush to push back his fur so he could see better, Ben suddenly appeared in the doorway. "Don't do that, Carrie," he said. "His hair is supposed to be that way. He's got weak eyes, and he needs the protection."

I said, "But he can't see well."

"How do you know?" Ben asked. "Stop worrying about it. Natural things are always right."

I remembered that then in the elevator, and I said, "Natural things are always right, Ben says."

That made my father angry, and I had known it would before I ever mentioned Ben. It just came out. The door opened at that moment, and he yanked Moon up to his feet. It wasn't like my father to yank anything, or to push or shout or get up angrily from a chair.

We took Moon to the park nearby and let him off the leash. He ran off to the bushes where it was too dark to see him, but I heard his tags rattling, the one for rabies and the license from the city. Sometimes there was a scrabble of his feet as he ran around among the dead leaves and broken bottles and newspapers. In the summer when the bushes leafed out and were green for a while, we couldn't bring Moon to the park. On summer nights, when it was hot and the broken glass winked in the patches of grass, the park murmured like a distant waterfall. But sometimes there were shouts and screams and the sound of police sirens.

My father hadn't said anything unusual yet and I felt myself waiting. It made me want to stand on my head, or throw a pie at someone, or laugh like a fool at nothing. He had something on his mind, and he was thinking about how to say it. I told Abby, I *swore* it, that when I grew up I would always say whatever was on my mind and not keep people on their beds of nails.

I kicked the hard ground. My father cleared his throat.

"Do you think you could ask Ben to not wear that leather ribbon around his hair?" he asked.

We were both leaning up against a tree. For a second, I thought the tree had begun to lean on me. I stepped out from under the leafless branches. Street lights glittered over the road that went through the park, and the brake lights of cars went off and on.

"I think I've got a sore throat," I said. Once I'd said it, my throat did feel a little sore. I knew that would get his attention. I knew he'd have to ask me some questions about that. My father is a specialist, a doctor for throats and ears and noses.

"How long have you had a sore throat?" my father asked in his office voice, so I told another lie and said an hour. I don't think he took it very seriously. Pretty soon, he stopped asking me questions and whistled for Moon. Then, as we walked into our apartment house, he said, "Carrie? Will you?"

"Well, I'll ask him," I said. "But he won't like it."

When we got upstairs, he looked down my throat. Then he prescribed a Hydrox cookie, and he smiled. I wished then, as I often did, that he was Ben's father too.

I finished my homework, including some I'd forgotten from last week. Then I put a chair up against my door and went to the closet where I took half a cigarette from my coat pocket. I closed myself into the closet and lit it.

I had smoked the first half of the cigarette sitting on my bed. And Ben caught me. He said I was a stupid little monster and snatched it out of my mouth and crushed it out in a souvenir plate I'd gotten in Chinatown. He said that if he caught me smoking again, he'd tell Mama. I said I'd never do it again, but I knew I would even while I was saying it. I don't understand how you can have two exactly opposite things in your mind at the same time and say only one of them is true.

The cigarette was so short I singed my nose and scattered sparks all over my shoes and on the clothes that had dropped off the hangers and were on the floor. After two puffs, I opened the door and swooped to my mirror. But I didn't look the way I'd hoped. I just looked crazy, lurching around the room with that crumpled bit of cigarette sticking out of my mouth. I looked like a used up Raggedy Ann doll I had had when I was little.

I buried the remains of the cigarette in the earth around my pepper plant, no doubt murdering its roots. I remembered the time I had sneaked a little wine and Mama had crept up on me while I was drinking it out of a coffee cup. "When you want wine, ask for it," she had said.

The next night, I asked for it at dinner.

"No," my mother said.

"But you said——" I began.

Then my father crossed his eyes and said, "That's life!"

I could hear Ben in the next room hitting the wooden headboard of his bed in time to the beat of a song he was listening to on his radio. I wondered if he'd take the rawhide thong off his hair when he went to sleep. I danced a little by myself in my room, trying to remember how Abby threw her shoulder forward for a certain step. I think I nearly dislocated mine. All the time, I was wondering how I'd tell Ben about the thong.

I didn't want him to get angry at me. Sometimes I felt like one of the pillows on the living room sofa, a pillow which each member of the family punched a little as he passed by. I didn't care if Ben wanted to wear a bicycle pump in his hair.

There were days when I thought Ben looked older than any of us, older even than my father. He looked so tired most of the time. But there were other times when he seemed my own age, times when he was eating something he liked or listening to music he loved. His face could change so quickly. As soon as anyone mentioned college, he'd look away from the person who had asked him—he'd look tired. He'd make up his mind soon, he'd say.

"Don't press him," my mother told my father.

"How can you press air?" my father said once. "When you ask Ben a question, he disappears." My mother said it was a blessing, at least, that the army wouldn't take him. He had something wrong with his right kneecap. He had had a bad accident when he was playing soccer.

Ben must have played soccer years ago when I was still a baby. I watched soccer games in the park. I couldn't imagine Ben ever looking like those boys, running so strongly, hitting the soccer ball with their knees and heads.

When I think of Ben, even when I'm looking straight at him across the supper table, I see a tall thin person in a droopy coat with the collar up. The person's hands are shoved into the coat pockets; the threads that stick out from the places where buttons used to be are a different color from the cloth of the coat. When he walks, the person looks down at his feet as they move forward in cracked muddy boots.

I got out a sweater and a skirt to wear the next

day to school. I knew I'd change my mind in the morning. Mama always says, "Lay out your clothes the night before, Carrie. It saves time."

Ben didn't look up when I came into his room. But at least the door wasn't locked.

Last year, he got rid of nearly all his things. He said he didn't want any clutter, so now there was only a bare oak table he had drawn on with India ink, a bed with his old blue camp blankets covering up the mattress, the headboard he'd carved his name in, the radio sitting on a wooden crate he'd found in the street, and two boxes where he kept his clothes, the bluejeans and workshirts all wound around each other like snakes. He used to have pictures on the walls, things he'd cut out of magazines, a calendar with photographs of cows standing in meadows, a big print Mama had given him of a man with a bandaged ear, a cartoon of a camel smoking a cigar. He'd thrown it all out.

For a while, Mama made up his bed on school days like she did mine, even though Ben had stopped going to school. But he wouldn't use sheets, and he said pillows were bad for your brains, so in time she stopped bothering.

"What's up?" he asked when the song came to an end. I looked at all the things he'd drawn and written on his table.

"Is that Chinese?" I asked, pointing at some bird-track lines.

"Maybe," Ben said.

In the middle of the table, he'd printed *Blowfish live in the sea*.

I looked at it for a minute. Then I got awfully mad. The announcer on the radio was screaming about records you could buy—Bargains! Bargains! $5 value for $1.98! Groovy! Groovy!

Why did he have to play that thing so loud it made your ears hurt? But what point was there in asking him? One day, last year, he came home from school and said he wasn't going back. From then on, it seemed, he'd decided not to say much of anything. "Hanging around," my father had said, "waiting for nothing."

I looked up and away from the news about blowfish. Ben was watching me. The rawhide thong dripped down his shirt collar. Ben looked dusty and sad. Sometimes I thought I loved him better than anyone.

"Why do you always write that about blowfish?" I asked him softly so he wouldn't look blank or get up and walk away. He bent down and turned off the radio.

"Because it's true," he said.

I didn't understand. I couldn't think of a second question. I stared at him. Then he smiled. "You have to start somewhere," he said.

"But whales live in the sea," I said. "And lots of other things."

"I'm not sure," he said.

"Why are you so sure about blowfish?" I asked.

"I've seen one," he said.

"In the sea?"

"Not exactly," he said, still smiling up at me.

I wanted to shout, "You're crazy!" But I couldn't to Ben. My friends and I called each other crazy all the time. I thought, I don't really know what it means.

"But why do you have to write it everywhere? I ,found it underneath a picture of Thomas Jefferson in my history book this morning. You even wrote it in my own book!" Then I remembered the time he'd spelled it out with cranberries on Mama's best linen tablecloth, and though she washed it a dozen times, one stain stayed. *That* was crazy.

He was slumped over now, like a tomato vine Mama would say when she saw him like that. I saw his hand reaching for the radio volume knob. Then he glanced at me and said, "I don't know . . ." He was looking blank.

"Please, Ben. Tell me?"

"Carrie! Lay off!" he said.

I hung around a little longer, tracing his India ink lines with my fingers. He tapped the headboard with his knuckles. I knew I wouldn't get another word out of him.

When I got back to my own room, I realized I hadn't said anything about the rawhide thong around his hair. Well, my father would give up. Mama would give up. What can you do with someone who goes blank?

I looked out the window, down to the street where the cars were driving back and forth. We were eight floors up so it wasn't too noisy except when the fire engines went by or the garbage trucks came, which is usually at three in the morning. Sometimes the garbage men woke me up, and if it wasn't too cold,

I'd lean out the window and listen to the men shout at each other.

I wrote Ben's message on my window with my finger. But the window must have been clean because the words didn't show up. It wouldn't have made anything clearer anyhow. I'd never even seen a blowfish.

Two:

A long time ago, Ben and I used to eat breakfast together, then he'd take Moon out for his morning walk. He never took the elevator—he said it was too crowded in the morning, full of zombies going to work, and he made up a story about someone he called Gluemaster who glued people together so they could go to jobs they hated. He said the glue began to melt in the afternoon, and by evening when all the people came home, they were real again, with human faces.

Now when I go to school in the morning, Ben is usually asleep, and I have to take Moon out. Sometimes Ben gets up, but he won't let Mama make him breakfast. One morning when I was eating cereal and toast, he ate a whole can of little green peas. Mama was trying not to look at him. She was standing near the stove, drinking coffee and holding back her hair with one hand. She gave me a queer look, put the cup down right on a burner and left the kitchen. My father said, "How are they?"

"What?" Ben asked.

"The peas," my father said.

"They lack a little something," Ben said.

"The right setting?" asked my father.

Then Mama walked back in and took the coffee cup off the burner. I think she must have been standing just outside the kitchen door. She said, "Oh well . . . it doesn't matter."

"Not as an isolated phenomenon," my father said.

"What?" I asked. "An isolated what?"

"Shut up, Carrie!" Ben said.

"Don't speak that way to your sister," my father said, dropping his spoon on a plate and standing up fast. Moon started barking. Ben got up and ran out of the room and Mama said in such a low voice I could hardly hear her, "All over a can of peas."

That was about the time Ben began to do a lot of things he'd never done before, the time he stopped doing things he'd always done.

For instance, he never brought his friends home. One week his room was full of boys stomping on the floor, laughing and shouting and hitting up against each other. The next week there wasn't any-body, nor after that to this day except for the night he brought a girl home to have supper with us.

She looked a little like him, perhaps because she was tall and thin. I hated her.

She was wearing a moth-eaten fur coat—"con-demned fur" my father said—and sunglasses the color of canned lemonade, and her big purple hat came down over her forehead almost touching the top rims of her glasses. When she took the hat off, I saw her little boney head all covered with thin shining slippery-looking yellow hair. She shook her head, and her hair fell down her back and flew over her shoulders like a cape, and while she was shak-ink her head she stared at me as if she were daring me to say something.

She wouldn't eat what Mama had cooked—which happened to be my favorite, veal and peppers. All she'd put in her mouth was a little salad, and pieces of bread she removed the crusts from.

Whenever Ben said anything, even if it was just, "Pass the butter, please," she'd smile down at her empty plate, her sunglasses winking in the light from the white globe over our dining table. My father acted crazy, talking to her all through sup-per as if he were having a real conversation. She didn't say hardly anything, just nodded or made little murmuring sounds.

"What are you interested in? What do you like to do? What are you going to be when you grow up?" Those were the questions my father asked, over and over. I knew what she was interested in. Ben. The rest of us were radio voices she could switch off by looking down at her empty plate. I knew her magic.

Just before Ben got ready to take her home, she spoke up very clearly. "My name is India," she said, only she said it to Moon, who yawned immediately.

After they'd gone, my father said she'd made up that name, and made up herself too. "You must try to be more tolerant, Dan," my mother said.

Ben never helped with errands anymore or any chores in the apartment. I used to get terribly angry, going to the corner store every day for milk and butter and canned tomatoes and dog biscuits, all the things Mama would run out of, or had forgotten, after her big Saturday morning shopping. So, for a while, Ben and I had terrible fights. But then he stopped fighting. I'd complain about having to do everything and would call him names. He'd just stare at me. I began to feel like a torturer. Abby said, "They're all alike." I guess she was right, although I think she was just copying her mother. Abby's mother is always saying that.

I don't think much about Ben during the day. But when it gets to be around two-thirty, just before the end of school, I start wondering what he's doing. I don't really know whether it's wondering or worrying. It started, I think, right after the night Ben ran away.

It was only a week after Grandpa died, in the middle of the winter. Mama said it was the coldest night of the year. Mama thought Ben would fall in the river, which was at least ten blocks away from where we lived. I told her he would have to dig a hole in the floating garbage to get down to water and she slapped me. Then she started to cry and sat down right next to the telephone. My cheek stung, and I was glad she was crying.

That week the telephone had been ringing all the time. Grandpa had gone on his yearly trip to Montreal to visit some distant relatives, and he'd died in his sleep in the house on St. Catherine Street.

There were all kinds of trouble because Canada is a foreign country and papers had to be signed and arrangements had to be made. Arrangements! The body had to be sent back by plane. The *body!*

I felt awful for a few days. Grandpa wore woolen vests and he was small and knobby and walked faster than I do. He smoked little brown cigars and loved coffee. He was Mama's father, and I think Ben liked him better than anyone else.

Until last year, Ben and my father got along

pretty well. And my mother always *worried* so about him. But he had a good time with Grandpa. Grandpa could make fun of Ben so that he'd actually laugh at himself. No one else could do that with my brother, not even in the better days when he was still happy.

Well, Ben came back the next morning. He hadn't run away at all, he said, just gone to a friend's house. I thought there'd be a lot of talking about his not having called up home to say where he'd gone. But there wasn't any conversation at all.

That morning I went into Ben's room a few minutes after he came home. He was staring out the window at the sky, which was gray and thick. It looked full of snow.

"What are you looking at, Ben?" I asked.

"A buzzard tree," he answered.

Lately, I've been wondering about Ben's father too. It's all so strange. I knew Mama had been little once. On rainy days when I couldn't go out, she'd get the photograph album, and she and I would sit on the sofa in front of the fake fireplace and drink cocoa and look at all the pictures. But they stopped when she was around seventeen. After that, there were just black blank pages with a few dried up picture stickers slipping around. Then I was born. She had a few pictures of Ben as a baby, which were all in a separate envelope. But she had none of Ben's father. I wanted to see him. I wanted to know what he looked like, and if he had smiled at her the way my father did in the picture she has framed, the one that sits on the table next to the television set.

"Does Ben ever see his father?" I asked her, as if I weren't living in the same apartment and didn't know *what* was going on.

"Not for years," she said. "Not since the day you were born, when Ben was six."

I wanted to ask her something else. I couldn't think what it was. But I felt embarrassed.

I wished my father would still grab Ben's arm and shake him a little, or throw an apple at him across the room, which would make my mother cry, "Oh, you'll break something, Dan!" Then my father and Ben would laugh.

Everything is so different now. I feel as if my clothes are all held together with safety pins and my shoes don't fit, neither of which is true. How could it all change back again? How could Ben start getting up in the morning again, or go to school or cut his hair or talk with me the way he used to?

Then it did change. Suddenly.

I had a Friday vacation because the teachers in my school were having one of their annual meetings. It was March, and I could smell spring coming.

I came home and barked back at Moon and threw my books on the floor and called, "Mama!"

She came from the bedroom. Ben was right behind her, dressed, with his hair tied up in the thong.

They both stared hard at me. What had I done?

"What's up?" I asked.

"Carrie, would you like to go away with Ben for a couple of days?" Mama asked.

"Where?"

"Ben's father has written him. He wants to see him."

"I thought you'd go with me, Carrie," Ben said.

I always say yes right away about going anywhere. But I felt stubborn and uneasy.

"Why?" I asked.

Mama looked at Ben, wanting him to explain. He picked up Moon and slung him over his shoulder, which Moon hates. Then he said, "I don't want to go by myself."

"Oh!" I said, feeling out of breath because I was suddenly happy. But when I looked at Mama, I knew she didn't care much for the idea of me going off with Ben. I wondered what my father had said about it, so I asked.

"I spoke to him at the office," she said. I imagined his waiting room with the grass paper that had turned yellow and the raggedy magazines and all the throats and noses and ears waiting to be looked at.

"The rest can go hang," he'd said once as a joke. But my mother said that wasn't so awfully funny. Ben said, "That's exactly the trouble with doctors." We were having supper then, and I knew everyone was going to get nervous. Pretty soon, people would go to their rooms and doors would shut, *bang* for my father's and mother's, another *bang* from Ben's, then my door that shut without a bang, just a kind of rattle from the broken lock the handyman never got around to fixing.

"He said you could go," she said.

I could tell from her voice that my father didn't like the idea either.

"Okay," I said. "I'll go. When? Where?"

"Tomorow morning," my mother replied. "Boston."

"How will we go?" I asked.

"Bus," said Ben. He held out a letter to me. He acted as though it were something he wanted to get rid of. This is what it said:

> *Dear Ben,*
>
> *I'll be in Boston for the weekend, Friday on through, and would be charmed to see you. It's been 11 or 12 years, hasn't it? I think we ought to take a look at each other, don't you? I enclose a modest check for getaway money which, I presume, your mother can cash. I'm staying at the Boston Traveler Arms, Room 348, and won't stir Friday morning, hoping for your imminent arrival. Can't wait!*
>
> *Dad*

My mother said suddenly, "How does he know you won't be in school?" as if she were arguing.

Ben didn't answer. I said, "Maybe he doesn't

know about school," and my mother smiled a little and said quickly, "That's likely."

"You're killing Moon," I said to Ben. "His head's beginning to unravel." Ben put Moon down and I went off to my room, where I took all the clothes I own out of my closet and bureau and spread them out on my bed. Then I called up Abby and asked her what I should wear to Boston, and she said, "Everything," and hung up.

Ben and I had breakfast early Friday morning, but neither of us finished the scrambled eggs. My father fussed at me so about finishing my breakfast that I finally said I'd throw up if I swallowed another mouthful. My mother said, "It's not her last meal, Dan."

They'd been up late last night; I'd heard them talking. Sometimes their voices were almost loud enough for me to hear, or guess, at what they were talking about. I remembered my mother saying, "We have to . . . we have to. Nothing is going to happen, just a short trip to Boston."

I suppose I felt strange about it too. It was the first time I'd gone off without either Mama or my father. I had stayed overnight at Abby's apartment, but she was on the fifth floor of our building so it didn't count.

Abby went to camp in the summer, but I never had. The four of us had always gone somewhere together in August, to Cape Cod or Tennessee or ' Deer Isle, Maine, and spent the time traveling around. In the fall we used to go for picnics in a park across the river. Ben was always allowed to make the fire. I remember him getting twigs and dumping them in my arms, and rolling up newspaper logs, then kneeling in front of the weak little flames and fanning them. Once when I was standing just behind him, and he was kneeling, I'd suddenly seen how much older he was than I, how much bigger. At that same picnic, a bird had flown right into our windshield just as we parked under some trees. Ben had leaped out of the back seat and run to where the bird had fallen. Then I'd walked over and found him with the bird in his hand, a little mound of smoky feathers.

"It's dead," he said quietly.

Ben had known everything then. I thought about that bird long after winter came, and Ben standing there with it in his hand.

At the front door, my father said, "Take care of everything, Ben."

Ben nodded and picked up our two canvas bags, then dropped them and went to the bookcase and took out a book without even looking at the cover and stuck it in the pocket of his old duffle coat.

"I wish you'd cut your hair," my father said suddenly .

Ben looked at the two bags, then grabbed them up but didn't say anything. I was kissed and hugged. I felt as if I was pulling *against* Mama and my father, so I really pushed them both away. The last thing I saw was their two faces looking after me, puzzled.

Three:

Ben headed for the back of the bus. As soon as we had poked our way there through the greenish darkness, newspapers rustling beneath our feet, he sank into a corner and took out the book. I wanted to sit next to the window but it wasn't easy to ask him to change seats with me.

I'd felt happy that Ben wanted me to go along

to Boston with him, but now he'd forgotten I was there. I picked up a damp newspaper from the floor and looked at the first page. In school, I was the environment reporter for current events so I never had to read anything except stories about garbage and smog and pollution. I had gotten quick about picking them out from all the others. After I had given some gruesome report about people dying like flies from smog, the teacher would say, "Very good, Carrie!"

This paper only had things about the war. The war had been going on ever since I could read, maybe from the time I was born, my whole life so far. People talked about it all the time, my father and Mama, their friends, the teachers in the school. I let the paper slip back to the floor and watched the people huddling through the door, carrying little bags and big pocketbooks and magazines. The bus was like a cave. Then the driver swung into his seat; he didn't look back, not even sideways. It was as though the only part of the bus he thought he was driving was just where he was sitting.

There was a great choking and coughing of the motor. The bus backed and turned like an elephant and we were out in city streets, pushing the little cars aside and snorting on down toward the highway. Ben was reading an old tattered copy of *Gulliver's Travels* which I knew had belonged to my father when he was a boy. I looked over Ben's arm at the page and read a few sentences, but I felt restless and not at all like reading. What if you had to live your whole life in a bus? Ben put down the book and stared out the window. Pretty soon his hand went up and he began to write a sentence of his own. I didn't have to wait for a shadow to hit the window to know what he had written.

"You ought to carve that on a rock in the park," I said.

"Maybe I'll make a song out of it."

"You might sell a million records," I said. "What would you do with the money?"

"Give it away," he answered.

"To me?"

"All right. What would you do with it?" he asked.

He was smiling a little and leaning against the window, so I could see his pale whiskers in the sunlight. He hardly had any, only what Mama called peach fuzz. My father had given him an electric razor for his birthday, but I guess he didn't use it much. I knew he had about a thousand pennies in the box the razor had come in, but I hadn't seen the razor in a long time. Maybe he took it apart. He used to take clocks apart and then forget how to put them back together.

"I'd buy a farm," I said.

"A farm!" He looked surprised. I was surprised myself at being able to surprise him. "Why would you do that?" he asked. Then he closed the book and stuck it back in his pocket and folded his hands together and looked at me. We were crossing a bridge, and far down below near the riverbank I saw a little train moving slowly back toward the city.

"With a stream on it," I said, "which I'd dam up for a few ducks and geese, a little polluted pond."

"Muscovy ducks," he said.

"And a barn with four horses."

"And a few cows," he said.

"And a couple of pigs," I said.

"And some bantam hens and a rooster," he said.

"No chickens of any kind," I said.

"Why not?"

"They're stupid."

"Carrie, they're not stupid. They're just what they are. Chickens!"

"Now don't start up about natural things," I said. "You know there's nothing dumber than a chicken. Just because it's natural doesn't mean it can't be *dumb*!"

"What about a goat?"

"Oh, yes! I love goats!"

"And dogs?"

"A farm dog for outside, a barn dog and a house dog. And a sackful of kittens, a kitchen cat, two cats for the barn, one for the shed. That's four, right? And a parrot, and one of those little donkeys I showed you in a magazine once."

"Would it be an old house or a new house?" he asked.

"If it's a farm, it would have to be old, Ben. With a big kitchen and a cellar and an attic. It would sit at the foot of a hill so the wind wouldn't rattle the windows."

"I don't think anyone would buy my song," Ben said after a moment.

I'd forgotten about blowfish. I was just sitting there in that crumby bus thinking about my pond with my ducks and geese floating around on it.

Ben and I used to talk like that, a long time ago, except when his friends were around, and then he wouldn't let me in the room. I guess he didn't want them to know about our game. The game was to figure out what we'd do if we had a million dollars. We used to play it all the time, when we were in the back of the car watching the motels and gas stations roll by, even sometimes at supper when my father and Mama were having some kind of conversation and not paying attention to us, while I was cooking up toasted cheese sandwiches for us, or sometimes through our bedroom walls. We always argued about whose turn it was to have the money. This was the first time we'd played the game for months. But it wasn't the same. He'd never given *me* his million dollars before, and he'd never *watched* me while we were playing it, watched me the way grown-ups often did so that in the middle of what I was saying, I'd suddenly hear my own voice and start feeling as if I was lying.

I looked at Ben. He was leaning against the

window. The game was over. I moved away from him. Except for us, the back seat of the bus was empty, because it was narrow and hard, I guess. I remembered the time Ben had said he'd use his million to buy a basketful of silver flutes, a tugboat and leatherbound copies of all the flute music that had ever been written. Then, he had said, he was going to get seven friends and hire a flute teacher. They would all live on the tugboat, and they would go from place to place on all the rivers and canals a tugboat could go on. They would stop at all the towns and villages and give flute concerts. I'd asked who was going to cook their meals, and Ben said a million dollars ought to be enough to hire a cook. The concerts would be free, he'd said.

I think he must have talked a lot about flutes in those days because, on his birthday, Mama and my father gave him a silver flute in a black case with faded purple velvet lining. Mama explained that even though it was secondhand, it was very good because it had belonged to a real musician who had gotten deadly sick and would never play again.

Ben always kept the flute on his table; sometimes he'd hold it up to his mouth with his hands stretched out along its length. He'd blow—a little windy puff would come out. Mama wanted him to take lessons, but he never got around to it. After a few months, he took the flute back to the store and resold it to the man who'd bought it from the musician. My father said that Mama should have made Ben earn the money to buy the flute, then he'd have learned how to play it.

"What do you think happened to that flute player who got deadly sick?" I asked Ben suddenly. He didn't know what I was talking about. "Oh, skip it!" I said. I hated the idea of having one of those conversations with Ben that was just like untangling a snarled ball of wool. Finally he'd remember, then he'd say, "I don't know," anyhow.

We stopped at a gas station where there was a little crumby restaurant. Ben and I had tuna fish salad sandwiches, and I had a chocolate malted. I finished the pickles on my plate and his. He made a face.

"Chocolate and pickles, ugh!" he said.

"You used to like them too," I said.

I must have gone to sleep for a while in the bus later on. When I woke up, I felt like Moon must feel in the elevator, just waiting for the door to open.

When it finally did, we were in Boston and I was feeling as if I'd been in a room alone for a long time. I asked Ben a dumb question then, just to hear his voice among all the voices around us in the bus station. "Where is the hotel?"

"I'll have to find out, won't I, Carrie? How would I know? Stay here in front of the clock and I'll go get a telephone book and ask someone how we get there."

It was just past twelve. I wondered if Ben's father, sitting in Room 348 at the Boston Traveler Arms, thought we'd gotten lost and weren't coming at all. Then I heard someone cry, "Oh! Oh!" in a loud sad voice. I saw an old lady bending over my canvas suitcase, reaching for her pocketbook which had spilled all its contents on the floor. She must have tripped. I got down to help her. She punched me right in the arm. I said, "Oh!" Then she said it, over and over again.

Such peculiar objects had fallen out of her big black plastic bag. A light bulb, for instance, and a pair of torn brown stockings that looked like spider webs, an empty perfume bottle, a lot of safety pins and a stiff cardboard picture of Jesus wearing a big red heart on the outside of his clothes from which drops of red fell. The drops looked just like the candy dots I used to eat on my way home from school.

"I'm sorry," I said, not meaning it really, but wanting her to look at whom she'd punched. She didn't answer, just shook her head and gave my suitcase a kick, then went her way. The people in the bus station were crossing back and forth across the floor, glancing at the clock, bumping into each other. A few were sprawled on benches, looking as if they'd been left there for a month with nothing to do except watch the people who still had full use of their limbs.

Then Ben came back and said the hotel was close by and we could walk there. I asked him if he'd called his father up to tell him we'd arrived and he snapped back, "Why do that? What's the point?" But at least his voice wasn't tired.

The air was damp and chilly and tasted of pavement, and the sunlight had gone. We made our way among all the parked buses and then found our-

selves on a little narrow street where glowing old-
fashioned gas lamps stood in front of the houses.
In that grayish city light, the flames of the lamps
looked sick, and I thought of hospitals. I wondered
why the gas wasn't turned down in daytime. Ben
must have read my mind. He said, "Stupid. See
how stupid it is! They have gas lamps but no real
lamplighters to come and snuff out the flames."

"They ought to use electricity," I said.

"They think if you have money you can even buy
back old times."

"I'm hungry," I said.

"We'll get something at the hotel."

"Aren't you excited, Ben? Seeing your father
after all this time?"

"Oh, Carrie!" he cried in such a loud voice two
men turned to stare at us. "If I had a million dollars right now, I'd make myself disappear."

Then we saw the hotel. It was gruesome. The
windows were dirty, and the torn awning over the
entrance was blotchy. A flap of canvas hung down
and shifted back and forth like a rag on a washline.
I saw a milk carton and an empty prune juice
bottle on a windowsill.

The lobby wasn't much bigger than our own living room. It felt like the place the bad weather was coming from, dark and stale and cold. A man was leaning over a long high counter, staring down at a paper cup. The people who were sitting in the shabby chairs near the windows were all old men; newspapers fell across their knees like thin blankets. One was snoring, his glasses on the very tip of his nose. Just as I looked at them, they fell off onto his lap, but he didn't awaken.

"Come on!" Ben said in a low urgent voice. We walked quickly to the elevator, where another old man sat on a stool. He was dozing, his chin touching the collar of his rusty red uniform. I wondered about the red marks all over his head. It looked as if he'd fallen on tacks.

"Third floor," said Ben. The old man sighed and turned a big lever from left to right. We creaked and whined upward, landing halfway between the third and fourth floors. "Now what?" exclaimed the old man, working the elevator up and down, trying to bring it into line. But at last the door opened, and Ben and I walked out onto a faded rug full of holes and patches. We were standing in a long passageway lined with dark brown doors. They looked like tombstones.

A bulb hung from the ceiling, throwing off a weak light. We couldn't hear our own footsteps. It was so silent, the air so still and used up. I shivered. It's strange how the emptier a place is, the more you can imagine hiding in it.

We found Room 348, and I waited for Ben to knock. But Ben had gone dead. I knocked, and instantly, Ben pinched me hard on the arm. I gritted my teeth so as not to cry out. "I'll get you later," I muttered.

"Why not now?" Ben whispered furiously.

"I don't want your father to see you beaten up by a girl half your age!"

Ben snorted, then banged at the door. We both did. But there was no sound.

"Gone!" said Ben. "Damn him forever!"

"Oh, Ben. Don't say that!" I cried. "Maybe he just went out to get something to eat. Maybe he went to get you a present."

"Stop trying to make it all right. You drive me crazy, Carrie!"

I felt terrible. I could have had a good time at

home. Abby and I were building a mouse city out of match boxes and balsa wood and bits of glass. There was a movie we had planned to see, and our parents had said yes, and I was going to go to the library and take out a big load of mystery stories because I didn't have any homework for a few days. Instead, I was starving to death in this graveyard while my brother was telling me I was crazy.

"Don't cry," he said. "I'm sorry. It's not your fault. I'm sorry, Carrie."

Neither of us wanted to take a chance on the elevator again so we looked for stairs and found them at the end of the hall. We ran down through crumpled newspapers and milk cartons and smashed cigarettes, back to the lobby. Ben went to the desk this time and asked if there was a message for him. The clerk tapped the desk with the empty paper cup, then gave Ben a long suspicious look. He dropped the cup on the floor, took a pencil and tapped his teeth with it.

"What did you say the name was?" he asked.

"Mr. Felix. Room 348. A message for Ben Felix. Me."

The clerk turned slowly and looked at the stack

of mailboxes. I didn't see any letters in any of them except one. The clerk drew that one out and stared at it.

"You're Ben Felix?" he asked, holding the letter behind his back.

"Yes. I said so."

"You got identification?"

Ben reached into his bluejean back pocket and took out an old wallet my father had given him. He opened it to show the clerk his social security number. I remember how pleased Mama had been when he'd gotten it two years ago, the summer he had a job as a counselor in a city day camp.

"I don't know that that's enough," the clerk said. "You coulda swiped that off someone."

"He's my brother, Ben Felix," I said, thinking the clerk was someone I'd really like to drop a custard pie on. Then I opened my pocketbook and dug around for my library card and bus pass and handed them over.

"Why isn't your name same as his?" asked the clerk. One of the old men must have decided something interesting was going on because he hobbled over and stood next to us, grinning.

"Because we don't have the same father!" I shouted suddenly.

"Billy. You just stop trying to be so important!" the old man cried in a squeaky voice. "Give that boy his letter! You don't give that boy his letter, why . . . I'll tear up this foul old lobby, tear it up to pieces just like I did last time!"

"Mr. Krakowski! Don't you threaten me!" shouted the desk clerk.

"Oh, ho! Then I'm going to start right now," said the old man, reaching for the hotel register where people wrote their names down.

The clerk dropped the letter and grabbed for the register. Ben picked up the letter and we both ran for the door. The last thing we heard was Mr. Krakowski just *screaming* with laughter over the clerk's shouting and the other old men chiming in, puffing and yelling. We ran a whole block, then slowed down in front of a coffee shop. Ben had the letter clutched in his hand, and he was actually laughing, not making any noise, but laughing.

We went into the coffee shop and Ben ordered 'us each a cheeseburger and big cokes. Mama had said to be careful about hamburgers in strange restaurants, but I didn't understand why since she'd just looked mysterious when I asked her.

' Open the letter," I said to Ben after the waitress had taken our orders. He took one of the knives she'd slapped down on the table and slit open the envelope. Inside there was a $20 bill and a piece of paper. Ben read it, then passed it over to me. I watched him fold up the $20 bill into a tiny square and stick it under the ketchup bottle.

The letter read:

> *Dear Lad,*
>
> *I called your mother this ayem to tell her that, alas, something happened at the ranch I run in Arizona. Some poor fool walked on a rattlesnake —something of that order. Low tragedy! Alas, again. I have to take the next plane out. But I'll phone you this weekend and we'll throw a new plan together. Plans, plans . . . they do go awry sometimes, don't they? I'm leaving you a little spot of money to make up for the boring bus trip. There are some good bookstores around this town, a really extraordinary glass museum somewhere near Harvard, or if you like, three movies (my own preference!). I'll see you soon in any event. Really, so disappointed for both of us! But soon. Very soon.*

The cheeseburgers arrived as I put the letter down. I didn't understand much in it—except that Mr. Felix had gone. The cokes were so full of shaved ice they were hard to drink. I started to lift up the ketchup bottle. The $20 bill slowly began to unfold without the weight to hold it down.

"He didn't want to see me," Ben said.

"But the rattlesnake——"

"Rattlesnake!" Ben exclaimed. "Tarantula! Scorpion! Red spitting cobra! Bengal tiger!"

"You'd better put that money away."

"I'm not going to touch that money."

"You don't have to," I said. "I'll keep it."

"Oh, Carrie," Ben said. "What would you do if you had twenty dollars?"

"We have got twenty dollars."

"He didn't want to see me."

"You didn't want to see him. You said, a long time before we even got to the hotel, that if you had a million dollars you'd made yourself disappear."

"That's different. It wasn't because I didn't *want* to see him."

"Well. Mr. Krakowski was glad to see us. I wonder what he did to that lobby last time he tore it up?"

Ben started to smile.

"Mr. Krakowski is a blowfish," he said.

Four:

There were two little rooms in the back of the coffee shop that were supposed to be bathrooms. On the door of one was a picture of a man wearing a top hat. It said BOYS. The other had a picture of a woman wearing a crinoline skirt, lots of curls and a big hat, and that said GIRLS. Mr. Kraus, my history teacher, had been telling us the history of plumbing

—he seemed to have a lot of feeling for plumbing—
and how you could almost measure historical de-
velopment by what he called the "facilities."

Those coffee shop toilets must have been built
during Babylonian times.

I read all the things written on the wall in lip-
stick or pencil or ink. If I'd said them in front of
Mama, she'd have sent me to my room for the day.
I'd heard them all before. There was one that made
me laugh and wouldn't have made anybody nervous.
It said: "You can't get there from here." That was
all.

I told it to Ben when I met him on the sidewalk.
He didn't think it was funny. He had his hands
shoved in his pockets, and his head was down so
that his hair fell over his face.

"Where's your ribbon?" I asked, feeling mean.

"It's not a ribbon, Carrie!"

We started off in the direction of the bus station,
passing through the street where the gas lamps
were still glowing. I told Ben a joke about a man
who dreams he has eaten a ten-pound marshmallow.
When he wakes up, his pillow is gone. Ben didn't
laugh. He grunted.

"Even Daddy laughed at that," I yelled.

"I know *that* old story," Ben said in a scornful voice, "trying to make your father laugh. . . ."

"I don't *have* to make Daddy laugh," I said. I was disgusted; Ben looked so droopy and stupid.

"Well, you don't *have* to make me laugh either," he said, as mean as I felt. We stood on a corner glaring at each other. People moved around us as if we were statues or a parked car. I thought of the long trip back home, probably in the back of the bus again, with Ben as silent as a wall. I thought of all those things I could have been doing instead of feeling damp and funny looking in Boston.

"We'd better call Mama," I said. Ben was looking down at the gutter as though he'd seen something valuable there and then lost sight of it.

"Human beings fill up the world with garbage," he said in his distant I-have-nothing-to-do-with-it voice.

"Ben, she'll want to know when to expect us."

"All the whales are dying," he said.

A man in a fuzzy hat with a feather stuck in the brim stopped to stare at us. "Whales . . . ," he muttered.

The bus station looked exactly the same. I was sure the same people were sitting on the benches, looking at the clock as though it would tell them where to go.

"Listen," Ben said. "Let's not take the next bus home. Let's walk around for a while. Maybe we could go to a movie."

"Well, all right. But we have to call her anyhow."

"What will you say?"

"I'll tell her we'll be home later. Could you find out the schedule?"

Ben walked to the information window. When he came back he said there was a ten o'clock bus. We'd be getting home awfully late, but at least we wouldn't have spent the whole day on buses. We both got out all the small change we had and went to the phone booths lined up against the wall. Two phones were out of order, and there was a very large woman squeezed into the third booth. I couldn't think how she'd gotten into it in the first place. She talked a long time, pressing her face into the phone, then turning to scowl at me.

"She's probably phoning someone to come and

help her get out of the booth," whispered Ben.

At last she hung up. Sighing and mumbling, dragging a shopping bag stuffed with parcels, she fought her way out of the booth.

"You oughta be in school, you oughta," she said as she went by us. "Looka that hair! Whyn't you cut that hair? What's so great about hair?"

I ducked into the booth and Ben took off for the magazine stand. The fat lady shook her great head and went to sit on a bench. I could feel her eyes on me. I dropped all the change just as the operator was asking me for it, and I could hear Mama's voice saying, "Hello, hello?" "Wait!" I cried, and then Mama said, "Operator, I'll pay the charges."

"Mama, did Ben's father phone you? About having to go back to his ranch . . . Mama?"

I thought the phone had gone dead. There wasn't a sound. Then Mama said almost in a whisper, "No, he didn't phone."

"Well, he wasn't at the hotel. But he left Ben a note and twenty dollars. So we thought we'd go to a movie and take the bus home later——"

"When?"

"At ten. But I can sleep on the bus. It's awful to come all this way and then not do anything. It's really nice here. Could we?"

"Did Ben feel very bad?" she asked, her voice louder.

"I guess he did," I said. I didn't want to talk to her about how Ben felt. I hated it when my father or Mama asked me questions about Ben and his feelings, what he'd said or done.

"He doesn't have a ranch. He's never had anything like one," she said. I didn't fall over with surprise. At the moment, it didn't seem important.

"Oh, Carrie! Won't you tell me about Ben?"

"Tell you what? Listen, we're okay. Just, can we stay a while longer?"

There was another long silence, then I told a lie.

"We haven't had any lunch, yet," I said. "We're both hungry."

"Don't eat hamburgers," she answered in a kind of dreamy way as though she were thinking about something else.

"Is it all right?"

"All right, then. We'll meet you at the bus station."

"Goodbye, Mama."

When I hung up, I felt as if school were over for the week. Ben was waiting just outside the booth, watching my face. I nodded okay, and we left that bus station in a hurry. I felt happy, excited, as though I was going to a party. Then I thought about the ranch that Ben's father didn't have. I get tired of keeping other people's secrets, especially my father's and Mama's and Ben's—keeping them all separate in little boxes in my mind. Someday, a high wind is going to come along and blow the lids off all the boxes and I won't know what to say to whom. I wished it would come along right then. I wondered, how did Mama know Mr. Felix didn't have a ranch?

Ben and I walked for miles, walked until my legs ached. We passed through streets lined with plain clean old houses, their curved windows covered by lace curtains. We walked up a little hill on a narrow street where the houses were tiny but the brass nameplates next to each door were huge.

We walked into a neighborhood where the streets were filled with big carts holding vegetables and fruit, where men wearing little hats shouted out things like, "We gotta fresha beans anda fresha peas anda cabbage anda fresh plum anda . . ."

Then we each had a piece of pizza in a small restaurant that had a sign saying "Grinders, Heros, Pizza Pies, Welcome Home Eddie."

"Who is Eddie?" I asked Ben.

"Home from the wars," said Ben dreamily. "Eddie came home. . . ."

Some streets looked as if they'd been forgotten by everyone alive; little houses, little empty stores, broken windows, a cat racing down dark stairs to a basement as we drew near. We stopped for a while at a book store where people stood as still as statues, holding books in their hands, and the owner, sitting at a big messy desk, smoked a pipe and read a book of his own. Ben found a tray of old maps. He showed me one of Greece. The edges of the paper were yellow with age and crumbled in our hands as we held it. Ben said the names of the towns and mountains were written in Latin. In the middle of a faded blue sea sat a fat little boat. In one corner there was a kind of star, and Ben explained it was a compass.

"Would you like to have this map, Carrie?" he asked.

I didn't think much of it—it wouldn't last much longer either—but Ben hadn't given me a present since my eighth birthday so I couldn't say no. Ben paid the man $1.38. The man put the map in an envelope he took from a pile on his desk. Then Ben handed it to me.

"Thanks. It's a beautiful map," I said.

"Okay," said Ben.

"I'm getting pretty tired."

"Maybe it's time for a movie," Ben said.

We found a street of movies, like the street of carts. The bright colored bulbs around the marquees looked pretty sickening in the gray light, like the gas lamps. The first movie showed shiny pictures of naked people smiling, as though daring you to mention they had forgotten their clothes. The second one was a war picture. The third was cowboys. That's the one we went to without even talking it over.

I felt terribly sleepy as soon as we got to our seats. The movie house must have been pretty old, it smelled so stale. Ben is shortsighted, so we sat down near the screen in a row where there were only two other people. One of them was fast asleep and snoring like a rhinoceros. For a minute, I thought it was Mr. Krakowski escaping from the police after having torn up the lobby of the Boston Traveler Arms. But it was just another old man.

I went to sleep, too, and dreamed about horses. Then Ben poked me and whispered, "You're missing the best part!" I looked up at the screen just as six men dropped dead.

It was dark when we left the theater, and I was hungry again. We went into another little restaurant and sat down in a booth. The waitress gave us a menu streaked with ketchup. I read, *Two eggs, any style, 80 cents.* Ben said he guessed we'd better start using that twenty so I handed it over. He asked me what I wanted, and I said eggs. He said he'd have the same. When you're tired, eggs are easy. The waitress came and I said, "Two poached eggs, please."

"We don't have poached eggs," she said.

Then Ben said he'd like two boiled eggs.

"We don't have those either," said the waitress.

"Then I'll have two eggs any style," Ben said, "And so will she."

After a while, the waitress brought us each a plate of fried eggs. Ben started to laugh. "Any style," he said.

"That's life," I said, just the way my father would have. We finished up with apple pie. The crust rose at least an inch from a couple of soggy slices of apple, but it wasn't so bad.

"Let's walk a little more," Ben said. "We've got lots of time before the bus."

I agreed right away. I guess the sleep and the food had made me feel better. Besides, I'd been afraid that at any moment Ben would go off into one of his moods where he doesn't speak for hours, sometimes days. He must have been feeling bad about Mr. Felix, yet he seemed to have gotten more cheerful as the day went on. I didn't want to argue with him about anything.

Boston looked better at night. A few stars shown through the clouds, and lights were on in houses so you could see people in their rooms. I felt a little like an orphan out in the cold, but I enjoyed feeling like that since I knew it wasn't true. A little boy who was peering out at the street waved to me, and I waved back. A few minutes later we came upon a large park, poorly lit, apparently empty.

Then I saw a few dark shapes of people moving slowly like fish in a dirty fishtank. A few were slouched over on benches. They made no noise.

"Could we go back and wait in the bus station?" I asked.

"It's too early," Ben replied.

A small dog ran at me, jumped up and licked my hand. I petted him, thinking of Moon, suddenly feeling homesick.

"Leave it alone," Ben said sharply. But the dog was dancing around my feet like a puppy. I didn't know what was the matter with Ben—he liked animals as much as I did.

"That dog's an attention freak," said a cracked voice nearby. I looked up at once. I could see the man's teeth shining in the light from a street lamp. He wasn't looking at me but staring straight at Ben. The dog suddenly barked, and the man shifted slightly so that his profile was turned toward me.

He had a nickel stuck in his ear.

"You want some grass?" he asked Ben in a low voice.

Ben started to brush past him but the man reached out and caught his arm.

"Gold, man!" he said.

My arms prickled. I took Ben's other hand and pulled.

"Let go!" Ben cried. "Let me go!" Who was he saying it to? I held on anyhow. Another figure glided up to where we were standing, a girl I thought, wearing a coat that fell to the sidewalk and wrinkled there like a rug wrapped around her feet. She had on one of those hats that came down and covered her forehead. I had the crazy thought it was Ben's friend, India. Then I saw the mustache, long and droopy. It wasn't a girl at all.

"It's like the best," said the mustache. Ben's hand tightened around my own. He pulled. But other figures began to rise from a nearby bench. I saw dark hats and manes of hair and feathers, mufflers to the sidewalk, and things that glittered. They all stood behind the man with the nickel in his ear. He was the general, and they were his army. He turned again, rapidly, and picked up the dog, which he held under one arm like a package. The dog wriggled, and the general thrust it out toward me.

"Want the dog? You can have the dog. . . ." I put out my hand and petted the soft fur.

"Carrie, move!" Ben said urgently.

The man began to laugh, the dog to bark. We began to run, veering across the street between the cars, racing past closed stores through slowly moving clumps of people, hearing all the time the laughing man and the barking dog. Ben let go of my hand. "Here," he said, and we ducked into a corner drugstore. The counter smelled of old egg salad, and a man in a tall white cotton hat said, "What'll it be?"

I felt as though I was still running.

"I think we'll have some coffee," Ben said. He was pale, and when he reached out to the metal container that held paper napkins, I saw that his hand was shaking.

Grass. I knew about that.

Ben had said, at the supper table to my father, "You don't know anything about it!" And my father, who seldom gets really angry, took hold of the edge of the table with both his hands. He said the Cenozoic period was one million years long and human beings had been asleep all that long time, until the very last five minutes of it, and then they had waked up and stood up and become human, and now they wanted to go back to that sleep again, to sleep forever and ever.

I hadn't known what he was talking about. I only knew he was angry and that my mother, staring down at her plate, was frightened. Ben had shouted, "Nobody ever listens to me- in this house!" and had gotten up from the table and run off to his room. My father had let go of the table and bowed his head, then looked at'me. "Do you know what we're talking about?" And I had said I guessed it was pot. He said what did I know about it? And I said a lot of kids in school talked about it all the time. "Talking?" he had asked. And I said, "Not just talking. Because two girls in the eighth grade were suspended from school because the math teacher caught them in the girls' bathroom, smoking a joint in one of the little cubicles." He said, "Carrie, don't you ever——" But Mama waved her hands wildly and said, "Dan, let's talk to

Carrie about this when we're calmer."

But they never did. And I never asked.

Our coffee came. I spilled half the pitcher of milk into mine.

"If I hadn't been with you, would you have bought the grass?" I asked Ben.

"Maybe."

"That man had a nickel in his ear."

Ben said, "To show he had hard drugs for sale. A $5 bag. That's what a nickel means."

"I hate you, Ben!"

He didn't move. For a second I thought I'd killed him. I wanted to shout that I hadn't said it, I didn't know why I'd said it, that there was a ventriloquist in the drugstore who had said it. I didn't say anything. The counterman was washing ice cream scoops in a sink full of gray water. An old lady came in, bought a pack of cigarettes from another man behind a counter and began arguing about her change.

"Sylvia, you do this every night. Now you *know* I always give you the correct change!" said the cashier.

Ben said, "I want to go back to the hotel. I want

to see if maybe he's there, if maybe he didn't go."

"But he *said* he was going to Arizona."

"I don't believe it. I want to go back to the hotel anyhow. I've got a feeling. . . ."

We each drank a little bit of our coffee. Ben paid the cashier, and we went out to the street. I kept looking behind me, but I didn't see the general and his army. Looking for them kept me from thinking about how tired I was, at least until we got back beneath that torn awning again.

The Boston Traveler Arms didn't look any better at night than it did in the day. There was a different clerk behind the desk, the old men were all gone, the ugly chairs, empty.

Ben walked over to the desk. "Is Mr. Felix in?" he asked.

The man looked at him suspiciously.

"Who wants to know?"

"His son."

The clerk turned to look at the stack of mail-boxes. The key for Room 348 was not in its box.

"All right. I guess you can go up," he said. He grinned, but it didn't make him more friendly looking.

We walked upstairs to the third floor, me about ten steps behind Ben. I could have gone to sleep in all the trash.

We went down the tombstone hall and came to the door marked 348. It was opened a crack. Ben put his hand on the knob, then looked at me.

"He's just a born liar," he said.

Five:

I thought there was a light on in Mr. Felix' room, but it was only a reflection from the street.

"Nobody here," I whispered.

There was a great growl from a dark corner, a giant echo of *"Nobody!"*

I heard Ben's hand brushing against the wall feeling for the light switch. When he found it, when

I heard the little click, I blinked and shut my eyes for a full second, then opened them, expecting to see I don't know what.

What I saw was a small thin man half hidden by the kind of chair people put out on the sidewalk for the junkman. He looked terribly strange. I saw why as Ben took a step toward him. He had half a mustache! On one side of his face, there wasn't any; and on the other, the droopy kind I had seen in a book of Ben's about early Texas when the bandits were running wild.

"Been shaving," said Mr. Felix in a gluey voice. "But somebody turned off the light." He grinned at us and seemed about to stand up, but instead sank back in the chair. Ben and I hadn't said a word yet. We kept edging closer to him as if we were playing Giant Steps.

"Not that I couldn't shave in the dark," said Mr. Felix. He sighed. "Of course, the absence of soap and water is inconvenient." He leaned forward, and a cowboy hat he'd apparently been leaning against slid over the back of the chair.

"Is it time for dinner?" he asked, and groaned. "Still another problem. . . ." he muttered, reaching out to a nearby table where there was a large, nearly empty bottle. He brought it up to his mouth and tipped it forward. He looked like an old baby.

Ben advanced another step and I followed.

"You look like General Custer, my boy," said Mr. Felix.

"You're drunk," Ben said in a low voice.

Mr. Felix leaned forward. "Not at all," he said. "Just resting."

"Do you know who I am?" shouted Ben suddenly. I jumped. Mr. Felix sprang to his feet, looked intently around on the floor, found his hat and jammed it on his head.

"Indeed I do!" he said in a fierce if slightly blurred voice. "You are the last of the Felix clan. And like the rest of us, you have no faith in the written word. Didn't I inform you I had gone back to Wyoming? How can it be that you don't believe your own father?"

"Arizona," Ben said.

"The difference is negligible," remarked Mr. Felix sternly.

"You couldn't have gotten all the way to Arizona and back in one day," I said.

Mr. Felix stared at me. "You have a legalistic mind, my girl," he said. Then he smiled. "You are my son's sister. I have heard your name, but it escapes me. Matilda? Alfreda? Bernadette? Gloriosa?"

"Carrie," I said.

"Good!" exclaimed Mr. Felix. "Let's find a decent restaurant in this miserable village and have dinner. My treat!"

Ben's face was red, and he was standing up very straight.

"Why didn't you wait for me this morning?" he asked in a stiff angry voice.

Mr. Felix looked at the bottle that had slipped down to rest against his black shoes. Then he touched the half of his upper lip from which the mustache was missing. He looked shocked.

"Good heavens! I've got someone else's face!" he cried.

"Why?" Ben asked again.

Mr. Felix removed his hat and studied it a long time.

"Well, the truth is," he began in a sad voice, "the truth is, Ben, I grew more and more apprehensive as the time of your arrival grew closer. It was wrong of me, very wrong. But after all these years, *all these years,* Ben! Of course, your mother wrote from time to time to tell me how you were coming along—school work, hobbies, so forth. To tell the truth——"

"Yes," said Ben. "The truth!"

"Scared, lad. Simply scared."

"My mother never did write to you. She couldn't have because she never knew where you were."

"Well, I had news . . . ," Mr. Felix said, his voice trailing off vaguely.

"You could have let it be," Ben exclaimed, turning away from his father and walking to the window. "You could have let it alone."

"A great urge to see you," muttered Mr. Felix. He looked hopefully at me. "I see Carrie understands. You do, don't you, Carrie?"

I hadn't taken my eyes off Mr. Felix for a second. I'd never met anyone like him. He was not like a father at all—at least, not like my father or Abby's or anyone else's I had seen.

I wouldn't have said so to Ben, but I liked Mr. Felix. I wished he'd leave that bottle alone. I had seen a few grown-ups who were drunk, once at Abby's house when I stayed over, and her parents had given a party. We had watched them through a crack in Abby's door. We'd decided they were gruesome. Then I'd often seen people staggering along the street in our neighborhood, especially on Saturday nights. And once I'd waked up at five in the morning and seen a man running right down the middle of the street, tearing off his clothes and yelling he was on fire. But Ben said, when I told him about it, that the man hadn't been drunk, he'd been crazy.

"Do you, Carrie?" Mr. Felix asked again. He saw me look at his bottle. He kicked it beneath the chair.

"Ah, well . . . why should you?" he said as if talking to himself. "No one knows. No one knows. . . ." I thought for a horrible minute that he was going to cry. Instead, he laughed. "Ben! Ben!" he cried. "We shall have a great feed and it will make new men of us! Summon the troops! Prepare to fan out over Boston!" He struggled to his feet and ran straight into the bureau opposite the two narrow beds.

"It's late, Ben," I said softly. "Mama expects us back on that ten o'clock bus." Ben turned his head slightly away from the window. I went over to him. "You go, Carrie," he said. "I've got to stay with him." We looked at Mr. Felix, who was now brushing his curly gray hair.

"I won't," I said.

"It's none of your business," Ben said in a low angry voice. Then he touched my shoulder. "Don't you start up! Don't you cry!"

"I'm not crying," I said, crying. "I don't want to go back alone." I felt all at once that if I left that hotel room without Ben, I'd never see him again.

"Then *you'll* have to call her. You'll have to tell her how we found him. She'll have a fit. She'll get so uptight she'll be here on the next plane."

"I'm upsick," I said.

"Don't make jokes. Just call her."

"All right. I will call her. I'll just say *he* came back and we're going to have dinner with him."

"Then it will be too late for you to go back. Oh, Carrie!"

"I'll go first thing in the morning."

"Where are you going to sleep? In the park?"

I shivered, thinking of the park. At that moment, Mr. Felix shouted, "Stop all that whispering! I've got half a mustache and am in no mood for plots."

I didn't know what to do. There was no one to tell me, no one with any sense. Maybe it was remembering the park and the general with his ear stopped up with nickels, maybe it was the feeling that things were going on in this room I didn't understand, but I got really scared. Mr. Felix was looking at the two of us, and Ben was staring at him.

"What's the problem?" Mr. Felix asked in a more ordinary voice than I'd heard him use before.

"Carrie wants to stay, and our mother's expecting us home on the ten o'clock bus," Ben said.

"Send her a telegram. Call her on the phone. Why shouldn't Carrie stay? I thought you had a *serious* problem, like my mustache. I must shave," said Mr. Felix. He picked up his razor from the bureau top, along with a small pink raggedy towel. "The accommodations here are not luxurious, although they are in excellent taste. The bathroom is down the hall. I'll try soap and water this time. Be back instantly." With that, he made his way carefully to the door as though there were objects on the floor he didn't want to step on. Rabbits, maybe.

"He's awful," I said as soon as the door had closed. I didn't really mean it. I meant everything was awful. Ben was writing on the window. "Stop writing that dumb thing!" I cried.

"Don't mess me up, Carrie."

"Then, stop! What am I supposed to do?"

"Take the ten o'clock. I'll stay."

"No."

"Carrie . . ." He wiped the window, then looked at the dust on his hand. "You're not scared of going back by yourself, are you?"

"No," I lied. I may end up being the worst liar who ever lived. But it wasn't just the bus trip going back that scared me. I wanted to see what was going to happen. I could just imagine Abby's face when I told her about that gross general and his nickel, and Mr. Felix with half a mustache. Mostly, I didn't want to leave Ben. I was hungry too. There were so many reasons for *not* going back that night that I almost forgot the one reason I should go back. Mama.

Ben was investigating the room now, punching the mattress on one of the skinny beds, lifting up a cushion from the chair, opening bureau drawers, picking up the bottle.

"What are you looking for?" I asked.

"I don't know," he said.

We both looked into Mr. Felix' suitcase. It was practically falling apart. There wasn't much in it, but we took everything out. I don't know why. There were a lot of matchbooks printed with advertisements for The Happy Hunting Ground Family Motel with Free T.V. There were a white shirt and some striped socks and pajamas with teddy bears running all over them. The pajamas seemed awfully big for that sort of design. At the bottom of the suitcase was a book, *How to Run Your Own Business*. Someone had written in black pencil, just below the title, . . . *into the ground*.

We put everything back. Then Ben said, "Okay. I'll call Mama and say you'll be back on the first bus in the morning."

"Me?"

"I don't know yet whether I'll go," said Ben.

"Oh, Ben! Ever?"

He didn't get a chance to answer, because Mr. Felix suddenly opened the door and leaned against it. He looked cross, and he was waving his hand at us as though he'd lost his voice.

"What's the matter?" asked Ben.

"Hand is shaking," Mr. Felix said. "Can't manage the mustache situation at all. Really! You'd think they'd devise special razors for this kind of problem. Who *doesn't* tremble?"

We followed him back down the hall to the bathroom. He kept to the middle of the rug, placing each foot in front of the other as if he were walking a traffic line.

In the bathroom, the toilet gurgled as though it were gargling. It had no seat at all. The sink was about as big as a cereal dish and there were lines of dirt in it like the tidal markings on a wharf. The bathtub's feet were shaped like dragon claws, and a line of paper books had been stuck between the tub rim and the wall. They looked soggy.

"This requires thought," said Mr. Felix. The three of us were very crowded in there. "Ah!" exclaimed Mr. Felix, and he stepped into the tub, shoes and all, sat down holding onto the rims and leaned back.

"This will give you the proper leverage," he said. "The razor's there on that shelf. The revolting yellow substance next to it is soap. I forgot my shaving cream in the haste of departure. I hope to heaven you've had some barbering experience!"

"None," said Ben. I thought I saw him smile. He found a sooty drinking glass, rinsed it out and put the soap in it. A trickle of water came out of the faucet, but he managed to work up a kind of slicky foam. He handed it over to Mr. Felix, who spread it over his entire face. Ben took the razor in hand.

"Wait!" cried Mr. Felix. "Remember! I'm your father!"

I started laughing. Mr. Felix shook his head, and said, "Wicked. Wicked, wicked Carrie." Ben perched on the side of the tub and began to make swipes at Mr. Felix' mustache, or what was left of it. Mr. Felix groaned frequently, but Ben's arm moved steadily. I leaned over as far as I could to see what was going on.

"This is the worst experience of my life," said Mr. Felix.

"Don't move your upper lip," Ben demanded.

I was reminded of the time I got chewing gum in my hair. I had to cut big chunks of it off, and Mama said I looked like I'd been attacked by predatory moths. The mustache was going, clump by clump.

A loud giggle erupted behind us. I turned, and there was Mr. Krakowski.

"Secrets!" he wheezed. "I knew there were secrets!"

Ben's arm flew up as Mr. Felix shouted, "Sir! This chamber is occupied."

"Chamber!" screamed Mr. Krakowski. He laughed so hard I was afraid he'd die on the spot. "Chamber pot!"

"You'll wake up everybody," I said.

"Exactly!" said Mr. Krakowski, calming down at once. "My life's ambition. This nuthouse ought to be scraped off the earth and flung into the Charles River."

"It's okay now," Ben said to his father. "At least it's off."

Mr. Felix was staring fixedly at Mr. Krakowski. "Good evening, sir," he said at last. "I hope you have a good night's rest."

"Not likely," replied Mr. Krakowski. "All these secrets..."

He moved out of the doorway, and I heard him walking down the hall, rustling a little as though his clothes were lined with newspapers.

Mr. Felix stepped out of the tub. There was no mirror in the bathroom so he couldn't look at himself. But he felt his upper lip. "Not bad," he said.

"I never shaved anyone before," said Ben. Mr. Felix put his hand flat on Ben's cheek and smiled.

When we got back to the room, Mr. Felix gave his room number to the telephone operator and got long distance. I thought he'd forgotten we had to call Mama, but I guess he heard more than he seemed to. He handed the phone to Ben and went to look at himself in the mirror.

Ben said, "Dan? My father turned up after all ... no ... we're staying the night here. In the hotel. She's okay. First one in the morning ...

but they run every few hours. . . ." Ben suddenly looked disgusted and pushed the phone into my hand.

"The whole thing is very uncomfortable for us, Ben," I heard my father saying. "You know how your mother worries. You should have——"

"Daddy?" I interrupted.

"Carrie. For heaven's sakes, Carrie, what's going on?"

"Nothing much," I said. "We're going out to have dinner."

"At this time of night? Do you know what time it is?"

"Well, Mr. Felix had some things to do. But everything is fine. I really liked the bus ride. And I'll be able to rest going back in the morning." They were always talking about resting. I thought my mentioning it might calm him down. He was silent. Then I heard Mama.

"Oh, Carrie!" she said. Along with being the world's worst liar, I began to feel like its biggest problem.

"Listen, Mama. We're fine. Just fine. Mr. Felix ——"

"I know Donald Felix," my mother cried. "It couldn't be fine. Carrie, I think you'd better take any bus you can get. You and Ben. Just come home."

Two hundred miles. I suddenly realized there were two hundred miles between Ben and me and Mama and my father.

"I'm too tired to come home," I said. "And I want dinner. Mr. Felix is really nice. He's taking care of everything."

"Donald couldn't——" she began. Then she sighed. "All right. But the first bus in the morning! Now give me your phone number."

I read off the number on the phone and we said goodbye and hung up.

"Your mother has displayed her usual confidence in me, I see," said Mr. Felix to Ben.

There were tiny patches of the mustache that Ben had missed. Still, Mr. Felix looked less shaky. He even looked a little taller, as though he'd been stretched somewhat.

It suddenly hit me that Mr. Felix and my mother had actually been married. They had lived in an apartment, maybe even a house. They had eaten breakfast together, and she'd taken *his* shirts to the laundry, hugged him the way she did my father, argued about money, made jokes, had a baby. Ben. I felt cold. Ben was sitting down in the ugly chair looking at the floor. But Mr. Felix was watching me. He smiled. "We are going to have a splendid dinner," he said. "Brush your clothes, brush your hair, brush your teeth! On your feet, Ben!"

I looked down at my dusty shoes. Mr. Felix walked steadily over to me. He bent down and kissed the top of my head. "Secrets!" he whispered.

Six:

When Ben is around, I don't usually notice other people much. Mama says that even when I was a baby, Ben was the one I kept my eyes on.

When I think of home, it's the place where Ben is.

This last year, I haven't much liked to think of home. Oh, it's always there, Mama and my father.

But so is something new Ben brought with him this last year. It is as though he made the house empty. Perhaps I began to feel this way when he threw everything out of his room. I remember the first time I saw his room after that, a square-shaped space with worn spots on the floor and cracks in the plaster and flaking windowsills. I wondered then if our whole apartment would have that same strangeness if we took all the pictures and furniture away. Of course, I know it would be *empty*. But I don't quite mean that. Ben's room gave me the feeling we were all just passing through. I even looked at school differently. I imagined the classrooms empty, all the children I knew gone.

The only place where I didn't have that queer feeling was the woods where we had our picnics in the fall and late spring. I knew that when we left with our picnic baskets and thermos bottle and car, the woods would still be there, unless all those stories I'd been reporting to my class were true.

I started thinking about how I always watch Ben because, for once, I was watching someone else, Mr. Felix.

He hummed to himself; he flicked a handkerchief

over his shoes; he investigated the inside of his cowboy hat. Then he flew at his suitcase, slammed down the cover, shook his watch, held it to his ear, glanced at the mirror, made a face at himself, punched a pillow, tweaked Ben's long hair, rushed to the window—all in about three minutes. I knew he was still drunk. But I guessed he was trying to make himself sober by all those quick turnings and bendings, despite the way he'd almost fallen onto a bed and had to grab a chair back.

In the lobby, Mr. Felix looked fiercely at the clerk.

"I want a room for this child," he said. "The best you have."

The clerk didn't smile or frown. He had a face like a blank sheet of paper. He turned and looked at the row of mailboxes.

"For how long?" he asked, then turned back to us.

"One night, tonight."

The clerk looked at his fingernails, which were bitten more than mine. He studied them like a jeweler looking at rubies.

"Abandon this pretense of thought!" shouted

Mr. Felix suddenly. "Aside from a few old rabbits without hutches of their own, this leaking ruin is as empty as your mind!"

"Kinely control your voice," said the clerk. "Kinely also control your temper."

"Okay," replied Mr. Felix in a normal voice. "I was just trying to attract your attention."

The clerk removed a key from a box and placed it down on the desk, then stared at it without speaking as if he expected it to crawl away. "Five dollars," he announced, keeping his eye on the key. "Single. Bathroom facilities down the hall."

Mr. Felix handed him a crumpled bill that he took from his breast pocket. The clerk smoothed it out with a flat grayish thumb, then handed a pen to Mr. Felix. He handed it to me and said, "You may sign for yourself."

I wrote down my name and address and the date.

"Now, let's cut," said Mr. Felix.

"Split," said Ben.

"I favor my own slang," said Mr. Felix to Ben, "although I would defend to the death your right to use yours."

We went out to the street. A light cold rain was falling.

"I smell spring in the air," said Mr. Felix.

"I smell a dirty city," said Ben.

"You take the pessimistic view, I see, Ben."

Ben didn't answer, and we all walked along in silence. Once more we came to the park. The general and most of his army gone. But I saw a few dark figures moving about uncertainly in the rain. They didn't seem to know there was a big park all around them, but stayed huddled together.

Mr. Felix began to speak, telling us that in the warm weather you could rent swanboats and float around on the lake in the middle of the park. He had seen people of all ages paddling around. "I've watched them at it for hours. They might as well have been sitting in boats shaped like tin cans. There they were, enthroned on beautiful floats shaped like swans with no expressions on their faces."

"Not even the children?" I asked.

"Well, perhaps the very smallest children smiled," he said.

Ben said, "I thought you spent all your time on your ranch—in Colorado or Arizona."

Mama said Mr. Felix didn't have a ranch. Did *she* know? I wondered.

"In between cattle drives," said Mr. Felix, "I visit the larger sinkholes of this civilization."

"What's a sinkhole?" I asked.

"Sewer drain," replied Mr. Felix. "I don't care for cities."

"Neither do I," agreed Ben.

I was walking next to Mr. Felix, Ben on the other side. They began talking together. I could feel them leaving me out, like two grown-ups. Ben was really talking, about farming and gardening, about something called an apiary.

"Apes?" I asked.

"Not apes," Mr. Felix said. "Bees."

Ben began to ask him questions about ranching. The words tumbled out one over the other until I could hardly understand him. I haven't heard Ben talk so much since the days we used to fight. He was walking fast, too, as though to keep up with his questions. Mr. Felix was having trouble keeping up with him. I followed a few steps behind. Then Mr. Felix stopped altogether.

We were standing in front of a place that had a sign reading, BA AND G ILL.

"Can this be a place where sheep and fish are sold? Or is it a bar?" asked Mr. Felix crossly. "I don't want sheep. I want a drink."

"No!" exclaimed Ben.

"Now, Ben, don't try to hustle me. I know what I want."

"We were going to have dinner," I said hopefully.

Mr. Felix sighed. "If children didn't require sustenance, they wouldn't be bad to have around," he said, but he did move on. "The Bostonians are going too far, dropping all those *r*'s," he muttered.

Ben's head was down and although I couldn't see his face, I knew he was mad by the way he walked, slow, scuffing his shoes. "Are you a drunk?" he asked suddenly.

"I'm not sure," began Mr. Felix, "that I consider that question any right of yours to ask."

"You're my father," Ben said.

"The right to practice cross-examination is not guaranteed to offspring," said Mr. Felix cheerfully.

"You didn't turn up until now. You lied in your note. We found you drunk. You never write. You don't know when I was born probably—or even *if* I was!"

Although Mr. Felix was wearing a cowboy hat, and Ben was speaking in a loud voice, no one paid attention. People were just paddling around us, in their imaginary swanboats, with no expressions on their faces.

"I hardly know my own birthdate," said Mr. Felix. "How should I know yours?"

"Irresponsible!" exclaimed Ben. "Mama's right!"

"Yes," said Mr. Felix sadly. "So she is. I am the most irresponsible man alive."

"Why do you have to be the *most* irresponsible," cried Ben furiously. "Why can't you just be ordinary——"

"That's a good observation," said Mr. Felix, cheerful again. "I do tend to be extreme. Now, here we are, The Golden Calf. Let us go in and worship. I hear it's the best in this bean Eden."

"It's expensive," said Ben. "I can tell by looking at it."

"We'll manage," replied Mr. Felix.

"I'd better give you back what's left of that twenty dollars you gave me," Ben said.

"Perhaps you're right. Caution, caution. . . . How would you like to be my business manager?" Ben snorted, and we marched in.

The difference between the lobby we had left and the restaurant we entered was enough to make even Mr. Felix look shy. Three out-of-work clowns, I thought. What I said was, "We look like sink-holes." Mr. Felix swept off his hat and stood very straight. "What people wear should be of utmost indifference to world travelers," he said, and took my arm and Ben's and pushed us into the softly lit room full of tables and gleaming glasses; thick brown curtains at the windows made the room feel even darker than it was. I was glad of that. I knew I was no world traveler. Abby would have probably thrown tablecloths over all of us. Abby even got dressed up to put the garbage out at the back door service entrance.

The only reason we were given a table, I think,

is because there were so few people in the restaurant at that hour. The waiter made an effort—I could tell by the stiff way he held his head—not to look at us. We were put right next to the door that led to the kitchen. Every time the door opened, I felt warmth from the ovens and smelled food.

Our water glasses were jammed with ice. The menu was as big as a kite. I would have settled for two eggs any style. Mr. Felix looked at me, smiled and pulled the menu out of my hands as the waiter poured water into our glasses. The little silk tassle that held the menu together touched my wrist. I heard the tinkle of ice cubes. For a minute, I really didn't know where I was.

"We will have clams and the filet mignon and a green salad and the apricot soufflé," said Mr. Felix loudly. The waiter lowered his head slightly, bowed to Mr. Felix' order and asked how we liked our steaks. Someone was watching us. Four pairs of eyes. Two empty tables away sat a family. The boy was about Ben's age, and his hair was cut short over his white shirt collar. The girl was a little older than me. Even in the darkness of the room, even though I could hardly see my fork and knife, I could feel those eyes.

"Observe that family over there," said Mr. Felix. "They're admiring us."

Ben laughed.

"They don't *think* they're admiring us. But they are. We have their attention. Attention is admiration."

"Not all kinds," said Ben.

"No, not all kinds," agreed Mr. Felix.

The waiter brought us oval plates of opened clams. Mr. Felix ate all of mine. He just looked at me looking at the clams and reached for them. He hadn't even asked me to at least taste them the way Mama always does with strange food.

"Send the sommelier!" Mr. Felix ordered the waiter.

"What's that?" I asked.

"The wine man," replied Mr. Felix. "We'll have a bottle to go with the steak."

"No," said Ben.

"You *must not* tell me no," said Mr. Felix.

Ben buttered a large roll carefully, then he

handed it to his father. "Please," he asked, "eat this instead."

Mr. Felix took the bread in his hand. He looked at it for a minute, then shook his head. "All right," he sighed, "if you feel that strongly about it."

The waiter had ignored Mr. Felix anyhow, so no sommelier turned up. We ate our steaks and salad, the waiter serving us like a pair of hands without a head. The dining room was nearly empty by then—only one old man was left. He had a book propped up against a sugar bowl. I was too tired to talk, not that I could have gotten a word in edgewise. Ben was doing most of the talking, asking his father about that ranch, how big was it, how many head of cattle, how many horses. Mr. Felix was eating faster and faster, his answers getting shorter and shorter. The soufflé came, and the waiter touched it with his thumb; it collapsed. "Couldn't resist, could you?" Mr. Felix muttered at the waiter.

Ben's voice ran down at last. I heard pots banging in the kitchen. The old man across the room closed his book and left; three lights went out. Mr. Felix drank the last of his coffee.

"I haven't got a ranch," he said, placing his cup gently in its saucer.

I looked quickly at Ben, but I couldn't see his face. I had known all along that Mr. Felix was lying. I'd done it myself. At first, it's easy. Then you get cornered, you contradict yourself. He'd spoken about irrigation, then about grazing, then about pigs, then about cattle, then about the north pasture, then he'd said Tucson, then Alburquerque.

The waiter brushed some crumbs into my lap.

"Listen," said Mr. Felix pleadingly. "I almost had a ranch just outside of Houston. I tried corn but the hurricanes laid the fields low, and the crows outsmarted me every time. Then I started raising gardenias. But they're too frail, hard to ship. I went broke. I tried shrimp fishing out of Biloxi, Mississippi. It was a bad year. I chartered fishing boats. I tried a little real estate in Florida. I've never cared for a nine-to-five life."

Ben was silent, looking into his coffee cup.

"I've always wanted to run things my way, outside, not inside, no walls *anywhere* where I had to look at them."

Mr. Felix suddenly jammed his cowboy hat back on his head.

"Listen, Ben!" he exclaimed. "It's a hard way to live, but I couldn't see the point of another kind of life for me. Once, when I was a kid, I thought of being a teacher. But even with those long vacations, I couldn't really do it. Besides, I'd hated being a student myself. Ben . . . there is such a thing in the world as not wanting to *do anything special*. I like weather, water, taking buses and getting off in places I've never been. I like to read books about the settling of the West, to find old tools or boats or cars that people have thrown out and fix them, polish them up, make them usable. I've got lots of friends, too, all over the country, wherever I've been. There's nothing better than hanging around with friends on a Sunday afternoon out in Minnesota in the woods, or on the porch of a little house on the west coast of Florida where the fishing boats are tied up right in front of you."

Mr. Felix seemed to dream. I leaned against my chair, wishing he'd say some more about what he'd done and where he'd been. Then he looked quickly at me, then back at Ben.

"When your mother and I were married, Ben," he said, "I decided to study botany. I don't know what I had in mind, maybe working for a tree nursery, something like that. When I was a young man, I got a job once working for the forestry service out in Yosemite National Park. Good heavens! What a summer that was! Nearly the best I ever had. Anyway, I started taking evening classes. But I had to work during the day in an office for a man who looked like a decayed elk."

"So you ran out," Ben said.

"Yes."

"You lie all the time."

"Just to you," said Mr. Felix. "I've never known how to explain anything. It seemed better not to try."

"Easier, you mean," said Ben.

"I guess so."

The waiter brought the check on a silver tray that he placed in front of Mr. Felix as if it made him sick. He turned his back on us but stayed close to the table. He probably thought we were going to leave without paying. Mr. Felix reached into his pockets, but instead of bringing out money, he threw some matchbooks on the table. They were just like the ones we had seen in his suitcase, advertising The Happy Hunting Ground Family Motel.

"That's mine. I run it. It was falling to pieces when I bought it, and unfortunately, the pieces are still falling. I've tried to do the painting and carpentry myself, but the wiring and plumbing defeat me. I've only got two out of six cottages in livable condition. It's right outside of Boston, on a main road. Promising situation, don't you think? There's a beautiful meadow just behind the cottages, although it's been used for a car dump the last few years, and the brook that winds through it is polluted. Just needs a little attention. I'm hoping to serve breakfast in the main house eventually. At the moment, there are eighteen busted beds in the dining room. But you can see what a good thing it could be, can't you?"

The waiter coughed insincerely. Mr. Felix piled up some money on the table, snatching bills from different pockets in his jacket. I thought he wasn't even going to look at the bill, just leave a pile of dollars the way people do in the movies. But he did look at it, then said quickly, "It was a fine dinner, wasn't it?"

Ben said nothing, so I said, "That was a terrific soufflé."

"I've had a terrific life," said Mr. Felix, looking at Ben. He waited for Ben to say something, his hands hovering over the money on the table. When Ben kept silent, Mr. Felix began to smooth out the bills and pile them up on the silver tray.

I thought of Mr. Felix' description of his run-down motel, his failures with corn and shrimps and the crows and boats, his friends far away in Minnesota and Florida. Would my father or Abby say they'd had terrific lives? I hadn't thought about my whole life before. I suddenly saw that Ben was smiling.

"It's not over yet," he said to his father. "And it may get worse."

Mr. Felix laughed wildly. Then he summoned the waiter and motioned toward the tray. He patted Ben's arm. He told me not to steal the restaurant silverware. "Let's get out of this silly place," he said loud enough for the waiter to hear.

I trailed behind them on the walk back to the

hotel. They talked about the motel, but I didn't listen. Too tired. In a way, I was tired of Ben and Mr. Felix too.

Later, when I was in bed, lying on a mattress that reminded me of a relief map of the Cordillera range Abby had made for social studies, I thought about the two hundred miles between me and Moon and Mama and my father. Before, when I'd talked to Mama on the phone, the two hundred miles had been on my side. Now, they'd turned against me. Each time my eyes nearly closed, I'd feel each mile like a little thorn in my side. The lamp on the bed-side table must have had a four-watt bulb. The whole room kept fading away, but I didn't want to lie awake in the dark.

There was a knock on the door. I got out of bed thinking it might be Mr. Krakowski with news about more secrets. But it was Ben. I hopped back under the thin blanket. Ben sat on the edge of the bed.

"Carrie, I'm really not going back with you tomorrow."

"You have to."

"No, I don't have to."

I felt scared. I felt I was about to fall over a cliff.

"Mama will kill me!"

"It's not your fault. It has nothing to do with you," he said. "I've decided to go to The Happy Hunting Ground." He smiled a little. "I wonder if he made up that name?"

"You mean, for good?"

"I don't know," he said. "But for a while anyhow. He needs some help to get it into shape. He doesn't have hardly any money. I think that dinner tonight just about cleaned him out."

"He doesn't pay much attention to money," I said, trying to sound scornful.

"No, he doesn't" Ben agreed.

"But what will I tell *them?*" I asked.

"You don't have to tell them much. I'll come back in a few days to pick up my clothes and my radio. I'll tell them then. You can say I'm just visiting him for now."

I wanted to tell him how much I'd like him to stay at home with us, how awful I felt at the thought of his not being there, even though everyone had been so nervous this last year, even though Mama and my father talked late in the night about him for so many nights, and I worried about him in school, and eating dinner together had gotten to be like rowing a little boat around inside a live volcano. But I didn't think he'd like to hear all that.

He'd taken off his rawhide thong, and he was winding it around his finger, sitting bent over, the way he sat at home. Ben.

"Okay," I said.

"Maybe you can come up the next vacation you have and help paint," he said.

My heart jumped. I saw myself in jeans, standing in sunlight near the meadow full of rusting cars and the polluted brook, painting away at the side of a building with a huge brush, great swashes of paint, a bottle of ginger ale waiting for me in the shade of the building, and Moon dancing around nearby. Mama probably wouldn't let me go.

"He told me he wasn't a bad cook," Ben said. Then he got up. "We'll take you to the early bus and see you off, Carrie." He stared at me for a minute or so. Then he said, "It'll be better this way."

Better, I thought when I turned off the light. People always say it'll be better when they do what they want. I had an imaginary conversation with Abby. She interrupted, and I fell asleep.

Seven:

We had breakfast at the bus station, doughnuts and coffee, and orange juice for me. Mr. Felix looked happy, but his hand shook when he dumped a load of sugar into my coffee.

"For energy," he said.

"I won't need much of that on the bus," I remarked.

He bought me a load of magazines from the newsstand, and chewing gum and Life Savers. His clothes were wrinkled, and his cowboy hat was streaked with what looked like car grease. I couldn't tell whether he liked me or my leaving. But I was feeling cranky and left out, ready to pick a fight.

They walked me to my bus. For a little while, I hated them both and said scornful things to them in my mind. They were talking about subjects that had nothing to do with me; it was as though I'd already gone. Just before I put my foot on the bus step, Mr. Felix leaned over and kissed the top of my head.

"Thank you for coming along, Carrie," he said. "I don't know how we'd have managed without you." I didn't know what he was talking about, but I felt better that he'd thanked me for whatever it was.

Ben squeezed my arm, and as he drew his hand away, I saw for the first time that it was a large grown-up hand. I don't even know if I actually said goodbye.

The bus ride was so boring, I don't care to think about it. The magazines took about ten minutes to go through. I stared out the window and saw nothing great, cars and motels and gas stations, now and then a little stretch of trees. Once I thought I saw a deer way off in the distance, but it was probably an escaped criminal.

I had to take another bus in the city. It was gray again, city weather. Pretty soon the forsythia would be blooming in the park, and for a week or two everything would look new.

They were both waiting for me. I didn't have to say anything to them for a minute because of Moon jumping up and down like a Yo-Yo, barking and licking my face.

"Where's Ben?" asked Mama.

"Have you had breakfast, Carrie?" asked my father.

"Why isn't Ben with you?" Mama questioned.

"You'll need a nap this afternoon, you look tired," said my father.

Then it got quiet. They were waiting. Moon went to fetch his rubber bone to bring to me. The phone rang, and my father went to answer it, saying he just had to get to the office.

I realized he would usually be there now, that he'd stayed home to wait for me.

I heard him talking to Miss Freeser, his nurse, whom he called "Cold Storage" when he was feeling comical. Then he came back and kissed me and said, "I'm glad you're back, Carrie." Meanwhile, Mama had been going through my canvas bag to see what needed washing.

It was better pretty soon. Mama made me some cocoa and toast, and she and my father had coffee. I told them about Mr. Felix and Boston. But not all of it. When I described the motel, and what Ben wanted to do, my father said, "It sounds like a good idea." But Mama shook her head and looked doubtful.

"Donald Felix is a gypsy wanderer," she said. "He'll come to no good."

Then my father said that Ben was old enough to find out about things for himself, and it was a good sign he had made the decision to stay with his father, and that my mother shouldn't interfere. Mama looked hurt, but my father got up from the table and said he had patients waiting, and pehaps we'd all go out to a movie that night after I'd taken a good long rest.

I telephoned Abby, and she said she'd be down right after she finished rearranging her clothes. I went off to my room and lay down. Moon got up on the foot of the bed, where he wasn't allowed, and curled up. I must have been tired after all because I fell asleep right away and didn't wake up until Abby appeared wearing a dress made out of crocheted string.

I told her all the things I hadn't told Mama and my father. For once, she didn't interrupt me. When I'd finished, she asked me to tell her again about Mr. Krakowski and the general with the nickel in his ear and the waiter in the restaurant. She wasn't much interested in Mr. Felix.

We did go to a movie that night, and I fell asleep right in the middle of it. School started up again, and Moon's morning walks, and everything was the same except for the emptiness of Ben's room, the silence at night.

He came home the next Saturday, walking into the house so quietly we wouldn't have known he was

there except for Moon's barking. I ran to hug him.
My father shook his hand and smiled. But Mama
was stiff and distant. She kept her hands clasped
tightly in front of her and hardly spoke.

Ben was carrying his own canvas bag and a suitcase that wasn't his. It had hotel stickers on it from
places all over the world, even Cairo, Egypt. I
knew it was Mr. Felix'. Later, when I went to
Ben's room and watched him packing, I asked if
Mr. Felix had really been to all those places adver-
tised on his suitcase. But Ben laughed and said no.
Someone had given Mr. Felix the stickers. But he
told Ben that if they made a good thing out of the
motel, they'd travel to those very hotels someday.
Ben looked up at me from the floor where he was
sorting out bluejeans and denim workshirts.

"You can't tell, Carrie. We might."

Ben looked pretty good. He was wearing Indian
beads around his neck that he told me his father had
bought for him in Boston.

"Are you painting the cabins?" I asked.

"Not yet. We've just started on the carpentry.
The place is a wreck."

"Why don't you call it the Blowfish Motel?" I asked.

Ben laughed out loud.

"Okay," he said.

I could see him painting an enormous sign, green letters on a white background, green for the sea.

"It's pretty good being out of the city," he said.

"Is he a good cook?"

"Well, not so bad. He had a job as a short-order cook in a diner once, so maybe he's a little too fast."

"Do you work all day?"

"All day. Then we go to the movies at night in Boston."

"Does he get drunk?"

Ben bent over the boxes, then suddenly turned them both over. A few marbles from long ago rolled out and under the bed. He pawed through his clothes. "He tries," he said at last. "But I don't let him."

Ben had lunch with us, and if it hadn't been for Mama looking sad, it would have been nice. My father was friendlier to Ben than he'd been in a long time. They teased each other in a way that didn't make me feel the toaster was going to blow

up. Then it was time for Ben to catch the afternoon
bus to Boston. He whispered to me that he didn't
like leaving Mr. Felix alone too long. Out loud, he
said, "I'll write you, Carrie."

"You might drop me a line too," Mama said.

"Sure," Ben said. "I'll do that. Carrie, I left
something for you. It's under my bed in a box,
a kind of present."

Then he was gone.

"At least I have his address," Mama said.

"He'll be back," my father said.

"Will he? For a visit once a year?" asked my
mother.

"Now stop that," said my father. "Do you want
him sitting at the kitchen table until he has a long
gray beard?"

My mother said, "Oh, Dan!" And my father
laughed. I didn't wait to hear any more but ran to
Ben's room.

Underneath his bed was a large square box covered with dust. I dragged it out and pulled the flaps
apart. A little note fell out. *My dear boy*, it said.
*Here's a little souvenir from the upper reaches of
the Amazon.*

I knew who that note was from.

"What's that?" my mother asked; she had been standing in the door, watching me I guess.

"A note from Mr. Felix," I said. "Ben said I could have what's in the box." My mother looked at the note while I took the newspaper covering off whatever was inside. I found the fish. It was as round as a soccer ball, stiff with varnish, orange and yellow and shiny. I knew what it was without ever having seen one.

"A blowfish!" I cried.

"I remember now," Mama said. "Donald Felix sent Ben that the week you were born. He bought it in some junk shop and wrote Ben his usual fairy tale about where he'd found it."

"The Amazon."

"The Amazon," repeated Mama. "Oh, that Donald Felix!"

"The Amazon is a river anyhow," I said. "And blowfish live in the sea."

My mother smiled unexpectedly. "I hope you're not going to start writing that on everything, Carrie," she said. She left the doorway and I sat on the floor, holding the blowfish. When I got up, I held it too tightly and pricked my finger. A small drop of blood appeared.

"I've been wounded," I said out loud. "I've been attacked by a dead fish."

I licked my finger and took the blowfish off to my room. I got out my writing paper and addressed an envelope to Abby, which I planned to slip under her door.

Dear Abigail, I wrote. *I've got a blowfish in my room.* I didn't sign it.

Then I put the blowfish down on my desk and looked at its open eyes.

"Ben?" I said, as a kind of joke.

I looked quickly at the door because I'd heard something, and I wouldn't have wanted anyone to hear me talking to myself. But it was only Moon coming in to find a spot of sunlight to lie down in.

I heard my father whistling in the little room off the kitchen. Maybe he was cleaning out our camp stove for a spring picnic. My mother was in the kitchen—I could hear the faucet running, a pan clanging on the stove.

Then I took a red crayon and wrote at the bottom of my note to Abby two more words: *Heh, heh!*

That would bring her running.